THE BEAR MUST GO ON

written by **Dev Petty**

illustrated by **Brandon Todd**

PHILOMEL BOOKS

Four woodland animals could not decide how to spend their spring day.

"I have an idea," said Rabbit. "Let's put on a show."

"A show?" said Bear.

"A **BIG** show," said Rabbit.

"The **BEST** show!" said Squirrel.

"**SHOW! SHOW! SHOW!**" said Other Squirrel.

WE WILL NEED COSTUMES
AND A REAL CURTAIN
A STAGE
AND INVITATIONS
LIGHTS
A SET
TICKETS
WE NEED MUSIC
MAYBE BIRDS
REFRESHMENTS
BIRDS WITH TINY HATS
A CHORUS OF CRICKETS

"And I will be the note taker!" said Bear.

"You don't want to be in the show?!"
asked Bear's friends.

"Oh, no," he said. "I'm much too shy."
Just thinking about being on stage
made Bear nervous. But he hummed a
little melody and felt like himself again.

Everyone was shouting over each other. "I need a **HAT**, that's very important. Write that down," said Rabbit.

"I also need a **HAT**! A tall hat. Write that down!" said Squirrel.

"Don't forget **LITTLE HATS** for the birds!" said Other Squirrel. "Hats with straps! Without straps their hats will fall off and the show will be ruined."

Bear gladly wrote it all down. He whistled a cheerful
little tune, happy to remain hatless backstage.

"VERY SHINY," said Squirrel.

"We also need tickets," said Rabbit. "SHINY tickets."

"Write SHINY in big letters, Bear!" said Other Squirrel. "No one will come if the tickets are dull. Everything will be ruined."

Bear surely didn't want anything ruined. He wanted everyone to come to the show, especially since he wouldn't be in it.

So he wrote it down, in BIG letters. As he did, he sang a sweet song, which made him smile.

Bear wrote, and he crooned the same little song.
He was fine with any curtain, as long as he'd be behind it.

Thankfully, everyone agreed nuts should be served.

Bear wrote down the list of nuts.

Together, the friends planned every
detail. The programs needed fancy writing.
The set would be painted in bright colors.
A drum, bell, and flute were absolutely
necessary. And seventeen rows of nine
chairs each, they figured, would be enough.

Bear wrote it all down.

The friends worked late into the night.
The sequins were sewn, the invitations sent,
and the hats hatted. Bear shined tickets and
sang aloud in the light of the moon.

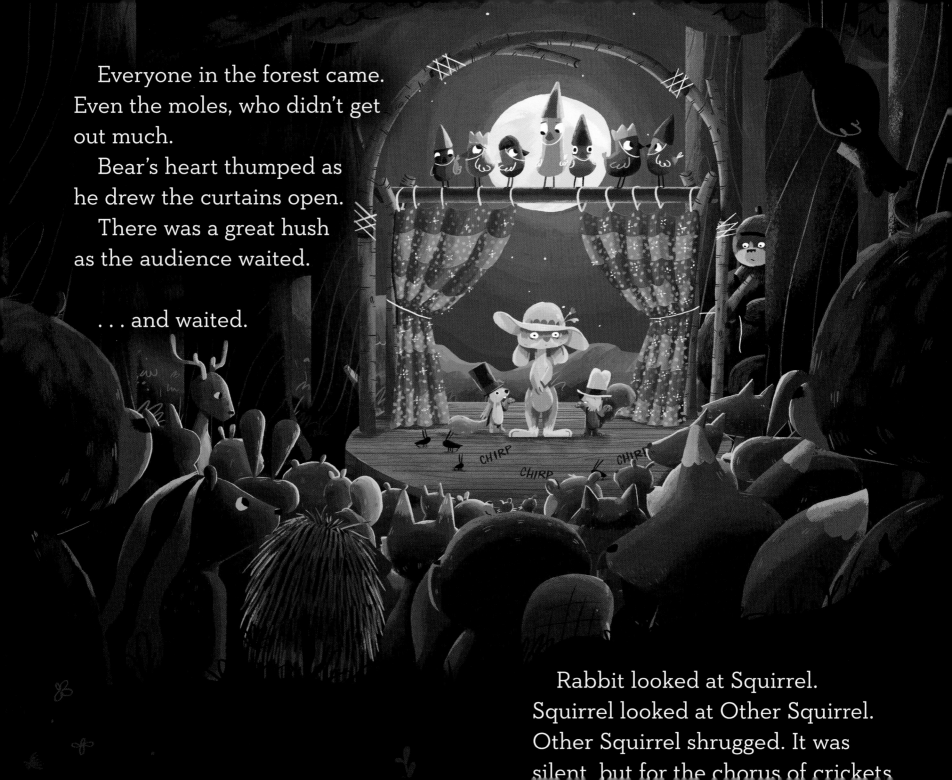

Everyone in the forest came.
Even the moles, who didn't get
out much.

Bear's heart thumped as
he drew the curtains open.

There was a great hush
as the audience waited.

. . . and waited.

CHIRP

CHIRP

CHIRP

Rabbit looked at Squirrel.
Squirrel looked at Other Squirrel.
Other Squirrel shrugged. It was
silent, but for the chorus of crickets

"Is it just me or did we forget something?" said Rabbit.

"Something important," said Squirrel.

"Did we salt the nuts?" said Other Squirrel.

"I'll check my notes," said Bear.

"Oh no! Oh no! Oh no! We forgot to write a show!" said Bear.

"What do we do?" said Rabbit.

"We're running out of time!" said Squirrel.

Other Squirrel was too worried to say a word.

But Bear had an idea.

"While we were working, I wrote a song. You can all go out there and sing my song!"

"But we can't read your writing," said Rabbit.

"And we don't know the tune," said Squirrel.

"YOU need to sing your song," said Other Squirrel.

"I can't," he said.
"You can," they said.
Bear looked at his friends. He could see
how much they were counting on him.

The curtain opened and Bear walked
into the spotlight. His heart pounded.
He thought about running away.

But he didn't.

He cleared his throat
and let his big bear voice
ring out across the forest.

It was beautiful.

In the end, the show wasn't ruined.
A song was written.
A bear found his voice.
And four friends brought the house down.
Sure, a handful of sequins came undone, some ferrets arrived late, one bird's hat fell off, and Bear forgot a few of the words.
But it turned out those things didn't matter at all.

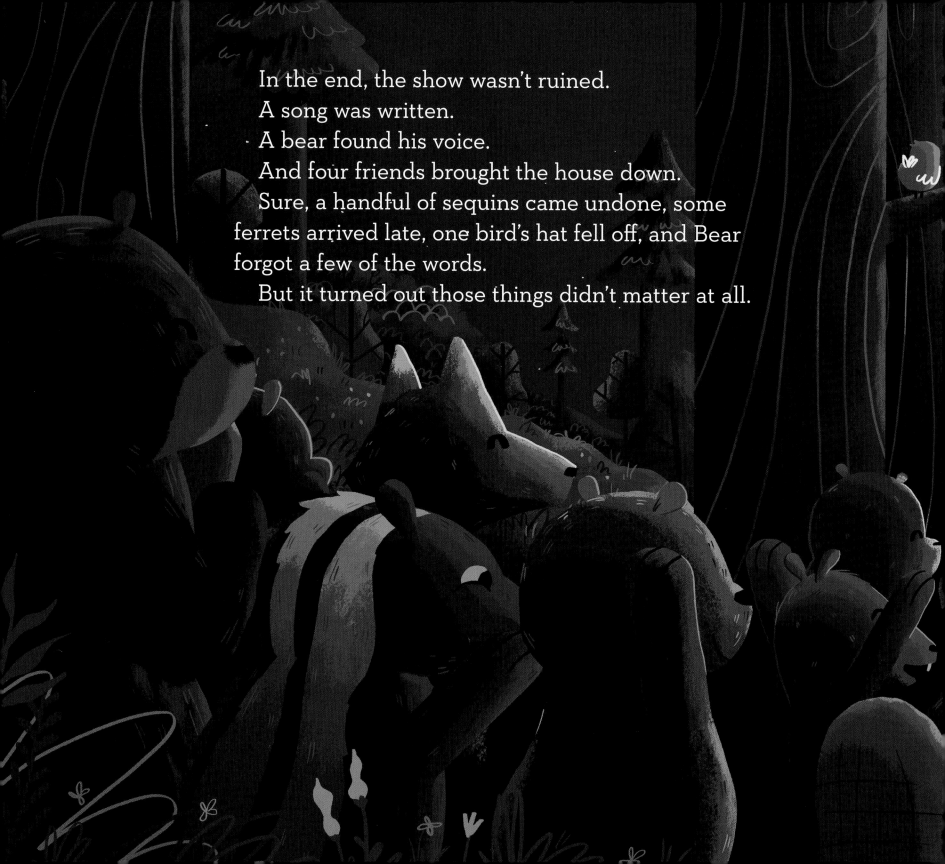

PHILOMEL BOOKS
An imprint of Penguin Random House LLC, New York

First published in the United States of America by Philomel,
an imprint of Penguin Random House LLC, 2020.

Visit us online at penguinrandomhouse.com

LIBRARY OF CONGRESS CATALOGING-IN-PUBLICATION DATA
Names: Petty, Dev, author. | Todd, Brandon, illustrator.
Title: The bear must go on / written by Dev Petty ; illustrated by Brandon Todd.
Description: New York : Philomel Books, 2020. | Summary: Rabbit, Bear, Squirrel, and Other Squirrel make big plans for a show, but they have
forgotten one very important thing and only shy Bear can help.| Identifiers: LCCN 2019018654 | ISBN 9781984837479 (hardcover) |
ISBN 9781984837042 (e-book) | ISBN 9781984837486 (e-book) | Subjects: | CYAC: Theater—Fiction. | Bashfulness—Fiction. | Animals—Fiction. |
Classification: LCC PZ7.P448138 Be 2020 | DDC [E]—dc23 LC record available at https://lccn.loc.gov/2019018654

Manufactured in China

ISBN 9781984837479

1 3 5 7 9 10 8 6 4 2

Edited by Talia Benamy.   Design by Jennifer Chung.   Text set in Neutraface Slab Text.
The art was created digitally.

For Susie, my pals center stage, and those in the wings.
Thanks for teaching me to love making a fool of myself for a good cause. —D. P.

For Tabitha, who nudges me out from behind the curtain. —B. T.